Mousekin's Lost Woodland

For Anne and David

Mousekin's Lost Woodland

STORY AND PICTURES BY
EDNA MILLER

SIMON & SCHUSTER BOOKS FOR YOUNG READERS
Published by Simon & Schuster
New York • London • Toronto • Sydney • Tokyo • Singapore

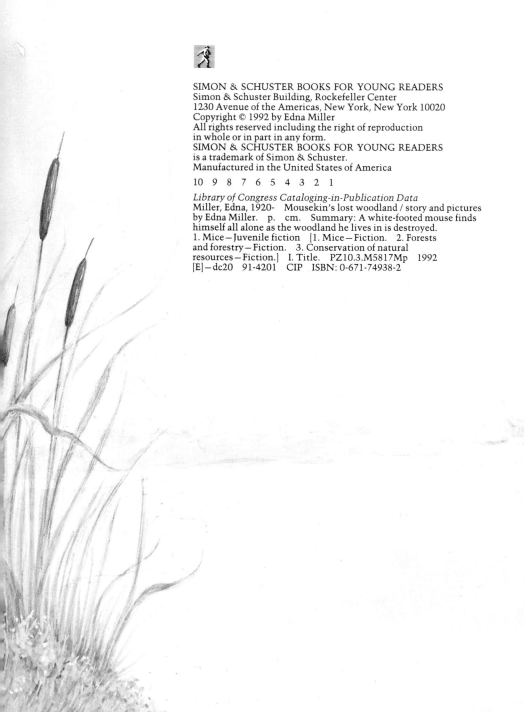

SIMON & SCHUSTER BOOKS FOR YOUNG READERS
Simon & Schuster Building, Rockefeller Center
1230 Avenue of the Americas, New York, New York 10020
Copyright © 1992 by Edna Miller
SIMON & SCHUSTER BOOKS FOR YOUNG READERS
is a trademark of Simon & Schuster.
Manufactured in the United States of America

10 9 8 7 6 5 4 3 2 1

Library of Congress Cataloging-in-Publication Data
Miller, Edna, 1920-   Mousekin's lost woodland / story and pictures
by Edna Miller.   p.   cm.   Summary: A white-footed mouse finds
himself all alone as the woodland he lives in is destroyed.
1. Mice — Juvenile fiction   [1. Mice — Fiction.   2. Forests
and forestry — Fiction.   3. Conservation of natural
resources — Fiction.]   I. Title.   PZ10.3.M5817Mp   1992
[E] — dc20   91-4201   CIP   ISBN: 0-671-74938-2

$\mathcal{M}$ousekin followed the marshy fringe
of a deep woodland pond.
He nibbled grasses at the water's edge
until the mist rose in the morning light
and the creatures of the pond awakened.

Beavers were the first to stir,
slapping the water with broad tails
as they swam to the distant shore.
They cut sticks and logs, and floated
them back to their beaver dam.

A painted turtle stretched his neck
to catch the first rays of the sun.

Mousekin raced to his cozy nest—
a craggy hollow in an old oak tree.
It wasn't safe for a white-footed mouse
to be about in the day!

As he snuggled into
the grass and leaves
that lined his nest in the tree,
he heard a buzzing noise.
It was much louder than any swarm of bees.
The oak tree shook and shuddered!

A squirrel family in the nest above
leaped for nearby branches.
A woodpecker flew from his nest below
Too frightened to move,
Mousekin crouched in his nest
as the great tree plunged to the ground.

All day Mousekin listened
to the terrible sound—
buzz-buzz-buzz.
He heard the crashing of trees all around.
He didn't see the one
who was cutting the timber down.

When evening came,
he crept from his nest
to find another home nearby.

He discovered an empty bluebird's nest
at the top of a wild apple tree.
Mousekin worked through the night
filling his house with the grass and leaves
he found on the forest floor.

No birds sang at the break of day.
The forest was strangely still
until one day he heard a familiar sound—
honk-honk, honk-honk.
Perhaps wild geese had returned
to the pond.

Mousekin hurried down the tree
and raced to the water's edge.
There would be feathers and down
to line his nest where the wild geese landed.

When Mousekin reached the pond,
he climbed a willow tree
to see how many geese
had landed near the water.
What he saw was frightful!

There were no geese.
There was no pond.
The beavers' house and dam
had been pushed aside.
Only a narrow stream of water
now trickled its way into the forest.

Mousekin watched as the other creatures
came to the empty pond.
A deer jumped down the dry, steep bank
to drink from the tiny stream.

A raccoon pawed the muddy water
for fish and frogs and polliwogs,
but they had all disappeared.

Mousekin hurried back
to the old apple tree
before the sun rose high.
He heard the honking sound again
as he hopped into his nest.
He didn't see the lumber truck
that was parked out in a clearing.

Mousekin woke one day
To another sound he knew—
rap-tap, rap-a-tap-tap.
Perhaps the woodpecker had returned
To build his nest nearby.

When Mousekin peered from his nest,
he could see strange figures
rapping and tapping
as a house went up in the clearing.

Mousekin watched as the land was cleared.
When the underbrush disappeared,
the rabbits did, too.
Chipmunks and game birds left to find cover.

When summer came,
the only sound Mousekin heard
was the roar of a mower's engine.
It crisscrossed rolling lawns all day
and kept the grass from growing high.

There were no sounds at sunset
when Mousekin woke to feed,
no cheerful peeps of tree toads
or murmurings of weary birds
as they settled down to sleep.

One evening as Mousekin searched for food
at the base of the apple tree,
a hand reached down beside him.
It grabbed a wild flower
growing near
and pulled it up
by its roots.

Mousekin squeaked in terror
and raced away.
He scrambled over the fallen trees
and past the empty pond.
He ran till daybreak lit
an unspoiled part of the forest.

Foxes, weasels, hawks, and owls
followed him into the woods.
(They were all fond of white-footed mice
and couldn't live long without them!)

Mousekin soon found a safe, warm nest
high in a beechnut tree.
It stood at the edge of a woodland pond
that the beavers had built anew.

From his high perch, Mousekin could see
another house built near the woods.
This house shared the land
with all the woodland creatures.
The trees were left standing
to shelter squirrels and deer.

Piles of brush were neatly stacked—
a cover for rabbits and quail.
There were bushes of berries
for birds and for mice.
Wild flowers grew beside small paths
that trailed off into the forest.